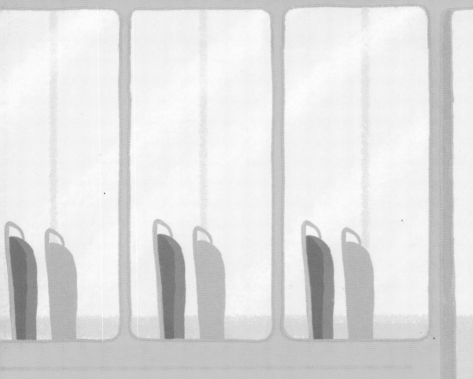

For Ruth – P.M.

For Olive – T.N.

LADYBIRD
An imprint of Penguin Random House LLC, New York

First published in the United Kingdom by Ladybird Books Ltd, 2021

First published in the United States of America by Ladybird,
an imprint of Penguin Random House LLC, New York, 2022

Visit us online at penguinrandomhouse.com.

Library of Congress Cataloging-in-Publication Data is available.

Manufactured in China

ISBN 9780241537619   10 9 8 7 6 5 4 3 2 1 RRD

THE DINOS ON THE BUS

Written by
PETER MILLETT

Illustrated by
TONY NEAL

The dinos on the bus go,
"Roar, roar, roar!
Roar, roar, roar!
Roar, roar, roar!"

The dinos on the bus go,

"Roar,

The teacher on the bus goes,

"Sit

down,

please!"

All through the land.

The feet on the bus go
Stomp, stomp, stomp!
Stomp, stomp, stomp!
Stomp, stomp, stomp!

The feet on the bus go

Stomp,

stomp, **stomp!** All through the land.

The raptors on the bus go

Pop, pop, pop!

Pop, pop, pop!

Pop, pop, pop!

The raptors on the bus go

Pop, pop, pop!

All through the land.

The bells on the bus go
Ding, ding, ding!
Ding, ding, ding!
Ding, ding, ding!

The bells on
the bus go

**Ding,
ding,
ding!**

All through
the land.

The grannies on the bus go,

"Shush,
shush,
shush!

Shush,
shush,
shush!

Shush,
shush,
shush!"

The dinos on the bus go up and down! Up and down! Up and down!

The dinos on the bus go,
"Eek, eek, eek!
Eek, eek, eek!
Eek, eek, eek!"

The dinos on the bus go,

"Eek,

All through the land.

The dinos on the bus go

Clap, clap, clap!

Clap, clap, clap!

Clap, clap, clap!

The dinos on the bus go

Clap, clap, clap!

All through the land.

The dinos on the bus go,
Yawn, yawn, yawn!
Yawn, yawn, yawn!
Yawn, yawn, yawn!

The dinos on the bus go,

Yawn,

yawn,

yawn . . .

. . . All the way home!